THE
APE MAN'S
BROTHER

THE APE MAN'S BROTHER

JOE R. LANSDALE

[SUBTERRANEAN PRESS 2014]

ISBN
978-1-59606-618-2

Subterranean Press
PO Box 190106
Burton, MI 48519

subterraneanpress.com

For Rick Klaw,
ape connoisseur

[1]

I am not a chimpanzee. I am not an ape. The guy who played me in the movie was an ape.

It's true. I did love that woman, that beautiful, blonde woman, and it was not a platonic love. It was much more than that. And in line with that, here's something I want to correct.

Because I'm not a chimpanzee, and am more accurately somewhere closer to an Australopithecus with a larger brain—which, of course makes me neither ape nor modern man, nor actually Australopithecus, but a humanoid off-shoot—what happened between the lady and myself was not technically bestiality, no matter what the tabloids say. But there was a crime. It was the breaking of the bond of brotherhood, and I regret it from the bottom of my heart.

Now the true events can be told, because other than myself, everyone involved with the sordid affair is now dead or missing, except that goddamn chimpanzee. He's got the constitution of a redwood tree. Then again it's not his fault. He was an actor. He was never actually involved, but the way he's treated, living in a retirement home for animals of the cinema, photos and articles popping up about him on his birthday every year, his fuzzy face covered in birthday cake, you'd think he'd at least have been President for a term.

Me, I was the real thing, and my raggedy ass has been left to its own devices. So, I thank you for coming to me to get the real story, and I will tell it true without dropping a stitch on the real lowdown.

[2]

It begins with The Big Guy.
The Big Guy, truth to tell, had few friends. There were some humans he liked, and many he tolerated. A few he killed. His true friends were that lovely woman, and me, who they came to call by a fictional name because of all those stupid movies. I'll not even repeat that name here. The whole thing makes me angry. The way I'm presented in the films, doing all those little tricks and throwing my feces—they didn't show that in the movie, and it never directly appeared in the books, but it's commonly known chimpanzees haven't any pause about filling their hands with their own mess and throwing it. Well, yes. I did it too. But that was when I was uncivilized. I have learned how to act, so that no longer applies to me.

I guess there's a little jealousy there, that damn ape stealing my thunder. But let me get back to what I was saying, and let me start with how I came to know The Big Guy. Forgive me if I trail off from time to time. I'm healthy, and all my external equipment still works, but my mind, though good, has many alleys, some of them blind, so I apologize in advance. Now, having come to a dead end in this alley, I'm turning about and coming back, looking for the light.

Let me start by saying I was there when the plane went down. Some accounts say it was a great sailing ship and that it crashed on a faraway shore, or that it was taken over by pirates, or that the child and his family were set adrift in a small boat.

All of these versions are false. These storytellers, these experts, also place events farther back in time as to when they really happened. This is partly so The Big Guy, as I call him, can be seen as ancient as Methuselah, but with muscles; a hero of folklore, not reality.

But, it wasn't a boat, and it wasn't a ship, and there were no pirates. It was a plane crash. We had never seen a plane, me and my tribe, and we had no idea that it had flown in from Greenland.

It looked like a great dragonfly falling out of the sky, buzzing and coughing and churning smoke, soon to explode. I know now, these many years later, that it was a small plane and it carried a husband and wife and baby. The parents were archeologists, scouting what they believed to be abandoned ancient ruins in the jungle of a lost, walled-in world.

They were right and they were wrong. The ruins were not abandoned. They were our home and had been the home of our ancestors for many years. Some of our culture had been lost, and the jungle had crept around the stones and swallowed them up and mossed them green. Our great scroll books had turned to dust. Our history was by then nothing but rocks, some scratches in the dirt, some huts, fuzzy memories passed on carelessly from the old to the young. Bottom line, we were pretty ignorant and there was a flea problem.

There were lots of reasons for our decline. No doubt we had fallen back into ignorance due to disease and human sacrifice. That sort of activity cuts down on the population. Offered sex organs were popular. Cut those buddies out and lay them on a sacrificial stone, set them on fire, and everyone thought the rain was coming.

But there was no rain for a long time, and there weren't enough private parts to go around for sacrifice, and by the time it was decided the gods weren't listening, or that perhaps they didn't have quite the taste for privates as were first assumed, half the population's genitals had gone up in smoke, and therefore half the population.

Our folk started disappearing into the jungle to stay attached to their equipment, and finally the sacrifice thing died out, and then the priest died out, and pretty soon we were eating bugs off trees and digging for grubs and trolling for anything edible that didn't eat us first.

Anyway, a lot of wing-dang-doodles were saved and we lost our faith in gods, which, though we were a primitive lot, put us way ahead of most everyone else in the world.

[3]

Out there in the depths of the jungle there was only greenery, and as seen from above I'm sure our primitive city was nothing more than a few flashes of white stone gripped in the clutches of moss and vines. Flying up there in their little plane they must have seen it and decided to come closer. But they came too close, and the top of a tree caught the bottom of the plane and ripped it.

I was young then, and I saw it happen from a perch in a tree. Saw the belly of the silver bird rip, saw it twist and spin and finally fall, spewing goods out of it like guts, throwing oil and gas like blood. It hit the top of one of our pyramids, bunched together like a wad of paper, and blew up, sending shrapnel skyward and amongst the trees in a hard, sharp rain. A piece of it killed one of my cousins, but I never liked him anyway.

The pyramid, the tallest one, the one the plane struck, was not Egyptian high or Egyptian grand, but it was well up there, and as I said, cloaked in moss and vines. From where I stood, even watching through the trees, I felt the heat from the blast of the plane lick at me like a baboon's breath, saw some of the vines curl and blacken, smoke and crumble. There came from the wreckage a horrible howl. All of us raced to the source, and as we came closer, I could smell meat cooking.

Then I heard a whine that turned into a gasping cry. There, lying on the moss-covered steps near the top of the pyramid, as if he had been placed there, was something I had never seen before. A near hairless thing, naked; its little bit of dark hair was smoking on its head. I ran over and beat out the flames gently with the palm of my hand, and lifted the thing high. It stopped crying immediately. As if in salute, it lifted its little pecker and pissed straight into my face.

●●●

Much has been written about The Big Guy, and I want to say right here and now, the one who wrote the most about him, claimed he was my man's main biographer, had no business telling the story in the first place. He wasn't there. But that didn't stop him. It didn't stop him from telling it wrong and making up facts and situations so he could sell a novel, and later profit from the motion pictures made from the series of stories he wrote about my good friend, The Big Guy. Well, we profited too, I have to admit. But I resent any profits he made. It was our story, not his, and he didn't deserve a single penny.

THE APE MAN'S BROTHER

First off, the name in the books and movies is way wrong. I can say the name but you can't. I can say it because it was given to him in my language. It sounds a little like a cough and a fart to say it right, but it is hard to repeat in human language. So, that's how he came to be known by the name in the books and movies and so on. In the books a monkey takes my place, and in the movies it's that chimpanzee. They gave the chimp a name close to my name but it's not my name.

Everyone now just calls me Bill.

●●●

So, here I am, holding this young human child in my arms, him pissing in my face, and all the others laughing. I admit, I was about to toss him from the top of the pyramid, when my mother, who had recently lost her child to some sort of jungle disease, comes up and takes The Little Guy from me and holds him to her breast. A moment later, she and The Little Guy disappear into the trees. I didn't know exactly what was going on. I thought maybe she was going to eat him in privacy, because it had crossed my mind to do just that. There wouldn't have been a lot of preparation and very little hair to spit out. Just swing him by the feet, whack him on a rock, and a hot dinner was served.

But mother carried him away from me, went swinging through the foliage. We can move amongst the jungle tree tops better than any human or ape our size. We are swifter than the chimpanzee because we are lighter, but stronger. I should also add that we have larger brains than the branch of humanity that survived. That would be you.

All I got to say is, "Good for you, you survivor you." But we were very good too. It was just fate that made you the main human branch and led to our dying out in the jungles of our lost world, amongst the trees and stones of our forefathers. If we just hadn't gotten religion for a while, no telling what we might have accomplished.

[4]

The Little Guy, who became The Big Guy, was a real whiner, and if mother had not been sad from losing my little brother to a hungry panther, he might well have been, as I stated, a nice hot lunch. But he clung to her tit with the enthusiasm of a leech, and her milk filled him and he grew.

Even when he was quite old for it, he still sucked that tit. I wanted to suck the tit, but nope. Only The Little Guy, who was hairless, and in my view a little on the ugly side, got the tit. Full grown, he'd come to the great nest in the trees, give our mom the fruit he had gathered, or the animals that he had killed, and before the feast, he would suckle. No one ate until The Big Guy was through drawing milk through the tit, and he liked to stretch this out, hugging mother, closing his eyes and sucking slowly, occasionally popping one eye open to see how the rest of us were taking it. The rest of us being my two sisters and myself. The best thing to do was to not look perturbed, but to just go about some business of a

[17]

sort, and forget it. He was more likely to quit that way and let us all get down to eating.

I will admit, however, there was something about him that made him special. We could all see it. We could all sense it. I would learn later that he had been the subject of an experiment. Dr. Rice, who you will learn more about, told me this. He never told The Big Guy. I'm not sure why. Maybe he planned to when the time was right. I don't know. But the time didn't get right and he didn't tell him. But I will come back to that later. What I know is this: His parents allowed The Big Guy, before birth, to be injected, right through his mother's stomach, with an experimental drug that was designed to give him elevated intelligence and great physical prowess and grant him an extraordinary life span. In the books his so-called biographer says this was achieved by the workings of a witch doctor, or at least I think he said that. As I was telling you, things are starting to slide off my brain like greased butts on a grassy slope. Important part is the injection worked. More on that later.

At the time all we knew was that he grew up to be tall and muscled and gold of skin and hung like a zebra. He could travel through the trees with the best of us, though he had to take to cinching up his snake with vines, least he catch it on a snag or drag it through thorns, something he once did, and something that took a couple days of careful work on my part to pull the thorns free. I don't know how I ended up with the job, but there you have it.

To say the least, this endeared him to me, and I to him. Why the latter, I'm a little confused. But, once again, there you have it.

He learned our language and customs quite comfortably. In time they were his language and customs, and he became my brother. He is still my brother, and will forever be. We lived a wild life, a good life, and there were many great adventures. We found lost cities containing civilizations thought long dead. We stole all manner of jewels and raped women with and without tails. Sometimes we did the men. This was just the way things were, so don't get highfalutin'. We chased creatures that your kind would call dinosaurs. We wrestled with saber-toothed tigers and wild boars as big as horses.

When they were in heat we fucked our sisters. Mom was off limits, being dry, but the sisters, they got to that time of the month we were all over that stuff. We couldn't help it. That was the custom. That was biology. We were no different than most jungle apes. I should add, technically, none of these sisters were The Big Guy's blood kin, and he couldn't impregnate them, and I fortunately never did.

By human standards we were stinkers. By our lost world standards, we were just growing boys. But even in our world, we had a reputation.

Watch out for those Monkey Boys (euphemism, I might add), they'll steal your stuff, whip your ass, and then fuck you. Hell, it's how we were brought up. As to who was referring to us as Monkey Boys (again, I'm using a euphemism), it was our neighbors, who were of our own blood, but who had branched off and taken up customs that we disagreed with, mostly having to do with hair-dos and the like. We killed off the bulk of them during our religious days, and the rest of them we killed off to have something to do when times were boring.

So, there we were, living in the jungle with our asses hanging out, our numbers decreasing faster than a baked pig at a luau, and then a little something happened that turned things around and gave us culture.

Well, it gave me culture.

What happened was HER, THE WOMAN.

[5]

One day me and The Big Guy we're out there in the depths of the jungle, beating an antelope to death with sticks, and we heard a noise that wasn't our antelope expiring, but was something else altogether different.

It was a melodious sound that reminded me of a bird. I often sat and listened to their sweet songs for an hour before I took a rock to one of them, ripped off the feathers and ate it, but this was different.

We left our dead antelope for the moment and took to the trees. Down there on the trail we saw a string of individuals, that except for the fact their bodies were covered in what I was to learn were clothes and pith helmets, looked a lot more like The Big Guy than me.

One of them was a delicate looking thing (actually she wasn't that delicate) with a long, blonde mass of hair bound back by a blue ribbon. At that point in time I had never seen blonde hair. The Big Guy's hair was black as night. But they had the same eyes—blue like water. She

had a bag on a strap slung over her shoulder, and when she stopped singing, she started talking to the man in front of her, a fellow with enough dark whiskers he could, at least in the face, pass for one of my kind. The rest of him, not so much. He was plump in the belly, which we are not. The way he walked was funny, and reminded me of how The Big Guy would walk from time to time when he wasn't climbing trees or moving about on all fours. Later I would learn this was the blonde female's father.

The Delicate Thing struck me at that moment in time as ugly as The Big Guy. Reason for this, I'm sure, is obvious. My view of what was beautiful was based on my upbringing, my culture, and my own appearance. My idea then of attractive was fur-covered, no sores, both eyes worked, they had a vagina, and the fleas were minimal, though sometimes you could eat fleas while you mated, which I suppose for us could be classified as a cheap dinner date.

In time my views on attractiveness changed. That's another can of worms, and I'll come to it.

But even then I liked the way she moved that butt. And I realized that though she wasn't making that bird-like sound now, it had been her voice I had heard, and to me in memory, it had sounded like music, which, except for clubbing a log with a stick and hooting wasn't something I was familiar with at that moment. I use it as a reference now as I think it can be more immediately understood. I was also thinking when she quit singing maybe we could club her to death and eat her same as the birds, peeling that stuff that covered her off the way we would yank out a bird's feathers.

Me and The Big Guy watched them from the trees, swung above them silently as they moved along the jungle trail. It must have been especially interesting to The Big Guy, because he had never seen any of his own kind before, not remembering his parents at all. I remembered them slightly, but only as crispy shells of cooked meat. I never did tell The Big Guy that a few of the tribe, one who will not be named, later partook of that flesh in a waste not want not attitude.

We followed them along, and it grew close to night. The moon was about half full, and shining through the trees. We could see clearly into their camp as they put up tents, built a fire, and so on. They had some long things with them that at the time I thought were clubs, but would later learn were rifles.

We watched as they ate from their supplies and went to bed. When we could hear them breathing deep in sleep, we climbed down and made our way cautiously on all fours toward where their packs were. We silently went at unfastening them, looking through them. Another trait of our kind is we're dadburn thieves.

What we found were cans of food, though we didn't know that, and we tossed those aside in favor of dried meat and fruits; the kind of drying used for keeping something way past the time it ought to be kept.

They had also, stupidly, left a number of their pots and pans they had prepared their meals in unwashed.

It was just the sort of thing that could call up a beast or one of us Jungle Folk. I found a kind of goo in one of the pans with chunks of vegetables I didn't recognize. I scooped it out on my finger and tasted it. I was suddenly aware—except for that one really swell meal after the plane crash—that what we had been eating was nothing more than grass and worms and ticks and stolen bird eggs and raw meat and such. This whole cooking thing was all right. You see, we Jungle Folk, smart as we were—and this is embarrassing to say— had yet to discover fire. And I might as well mention that we hadn't found out about the wheel either, or the missionary position.

So, me and The Big Guy are licking pans, and all of a sudden, The Woman is standing there. Next thing I know she's jabbering in a language that at that point in time I didn't understand. But I knew enough from her tone to know what she had to say wasn't pleasant and had something to do with us.

Next thing I know The Big Guy is walking up to her. He had a look on his face like he had just been born and was seeing the world for the first time. He reached out to touch her, and she gave him a kick in the old melons that would have made an elephant go to its knees. Damn sure made The Big Guy drop. Strangely, he had a smile on his face when he looked up at her.

Frankly, she had me feeling a might warm and contented myself. I wasn't sure why a non-hairy, clothed female should make me feel that way, but she did. And to reiterate, I never was quite the same for the hairy women folk of my tribe after that.

I had seen gold and I no longer wanted silver.

[6]

I have to go backwards a little, because as I said before, I tend to wander. But I should say that where we lived in that deep jungle was a kind of bowl. It dipped deep down on the sides and went wide, and as far as we knew, there was no way out. It was miles and miles across, in all directions. If we climbed up any one of the sides, moving through the trees, eventually, the trees played out. When that happened there were some rocks to climb, and caves, if you were willing to go up that high. There were nasty things that roosted in those caves and they had lots of teeth and could fly, so we were extra careful. Finally, above that, there were straight slick walls, all around, and way up for miles. And when I say slick, I mean slick. The stone that made up the walls was like glass, and often damp. It wouldn't even hold moss that you could grab onto. There was no way to climb. For us, that deep bowl of jungle, and all it contained, was it. A plane flying over might not even know what it was looking at, with all that jungle hiding what was down below, and the fact that a mist rolled high and over most of it much of the time like a roof of sun-leaking cotton.

At one time, Dr. Rice (and you will soon know who he is) in his zeppelin, exploring, saw our world. He had made an aerial expedition all the way from New York City, based on old records written by an Italian sailing captain and navigator who claimed to have found a large island, possibly a continent, rising out of the ocean. It was thought for centuries to be a myth, or an incorrect sighting of some known land, but Dr. Rice had taken it seriously and flown over our world by zeppelin, feeling sure that through the mist he had seen a flash of green, lush land. He told his colleagues, The Big Guy's parents, and they thought they could follow Dr. Rice's navigational information, fly out of Greenland, but the navigational charts were off, or they misread them. It was a longer trip than they expected. Even though they wouldn't have had enough fuel to return, they made it to our world, had seen the ruins of our civilization, and were most likely looking for some place to land when the accident happened that turned them from archeologist to well-done with no sides.

I learned all this later, of course. Dr. Rice's guilty feelings about his report leading to The Big Guy's parents trying to come to our world and losing their lives, led to his coming back on a possible rescue expedition, something it took him years to finance. He had hopes they and their baby son might have survived, some nineteen years later by the way they calculated time.

But, there we were, me and The Big Guy, The Woman having caught us in their pans. She was mad, surprised, and there was sweat on her forehead, her hair coming loose from being tied back, falling on her cheeks and neck, one leg bent forward, the back leg ready for another kick.

The Big Guy, the most powerful being I have ever seen, was on the ground holding his melons like he was testing them to see how ripe they were. Me, I'm just standing there grinning. My race is like that. We grin. It may look friendly, and sometimes it is, but it's a grin that can mean a lot of different things. From, how about you and me go over in the bushes, to I'm about to bite your face off, or how about we share that dead snake. Even we have trouble sorting out meanings from time to time, and mistakes are sometimes made.

So, there we stood.

That's when one of the men, a tall, flame-headed one, came running up, pointing one of those clubs at me. I'm thinking he can't do much business with it, the way he's holding it, part of it tucked against his shoulder and all. And then The Woman hits the end of it and the club goes up and barks, and fire comes out of the tip of it, and something rattles off in the bushes, like a rock has been thrown, and an suspecting monkey falls dead out of a tree without so much as a squeak.

I shit all over the place. It's not an unnatural reaction to fear, I might add. It's just I didn't know it was unseemly or might even be thought of as cowardly by those of your race, so I just let it fly. There's a comfort in it, and I want to add promptly that though I had this problem for quite some time, and the chimpanzee that played me in the movies certainly had some similarities, I was quickly civilized on the matter. I know. I've brought this up before, but I'm bothered by it, and I want people to know I've moved on from my primitive state, and though I'm a little embarrassed by the subject, I feel it is only fair that I trudge ahead and be honest and stress my developmental growth.

Next thing I knew, The Big Guy was up, and stirring. He could always recover from something bad quicker than anyone I have ever known. He grabbed that banging club and jerked it out of that man's hands and hit him in the head with it, knocked him down. Then he held it by what I now know to be the stock of the rifle, and grabbed the barrel, and he bent that barrel like it was a green vine. Bent it and tossed it into the greenery. Damn if he didn't bang another monkey. It fell out of the undergrowth and into the moonlight and thrashed around on the ground, then sort of crawled off to cover inside a flowered bush and quivered for awhile before it went still. It was not a good day for monkeys.

All the others of The Woman's group came running up then. They all had the same kind of clubs. They were pointing them at us. During all this action, I had rushed up beside The Big Guy. I thought it was going to be a fight to the death, and I was more than willing, maybe even a little anxious to try it out, see how we'd fare against all those men. I had no idea about the guns, then. I had heard one, and I had seen it spit fire, but I didn't know they threw bullets. I thought that first monkey had just fainted at the sound of the shot. I thought it would be us against them, arms against arms, legs against legs, fists against fists, skulls against skulls, and their clubs against us. But, of course, that isn't how it would have been. That many armed men, no matter how strong and quick The Big Guy was, no matter how savage the both of us were, we'd have lasted just about long enough for our balls to swing once between our legs before we hit the ground, torn apart by bullets. What saved us was The Woman raised her hand and yelled at the others. Everything stopped. She stood staring at The Big Guy, and he stood staring at her.

The Big Guy had never seen anything like her, all curved up in the right places, wet, red lips and shiny blue eyes. And she was looking at a very big man with dark hair and a body that was all long, lean muscle, dirt and scars and deep suntan; from the way her face relaxed, I had a pretty good idea she liked what she was looking at as much as he liked what he was looking at.

It was while they were looking at one another, The Woman with her arm raised, holding back action from those behind her, that there was a screech loud enough to make my backbone shift. A great shadow flowed across the moon and a flying, feathered lizard as big as one of your air planes, swooped down and grabbed The Woman by hooking its claws in her shoulder.

Those damn things were all over our part of the world. A nuisance is what they were. So, it was pretty much over for The Woman, I thought, and then the next thing I know The Big Guy is running. I mean, he is moving. He took to one of the tall trees, and went up it swiftly. Those flying creatures have an odd habit of grabbing something, then circling back, maybe to see if they've left part of it on the ground. This habit was something The Big Guy, of course, was fully acquainted with, and he took advantage of it.

It was circling back, true to from, and The Big Guy having judged its circle had quickly climbed that tree, and as the thing winged by, The Big Guy leaped and effortlessly landed on its back. He wrapped one arm around its neck, went to beating its hard head with his free fist. You could hear him whapping it all the way from where we stood.

As the thing flew over us, blood sprinkled down on us from the The Big Guy's blows, that and brains from that thing, and the next thing you know, its crashing into a tree, and letting go of The Woman. The Big Guy, moving faster than a snake can strike, leaped off that flying, twisting, falling wreck, grabbed The Woman's arm as he went, and swung them both into the leafy boughs of the tree.

There they were, standing on a limb in a tall tree, her shoulder slightly wet with blood, bleeding through the cloth of her torn shirt, and there he was, standing without clothes, staring into her eyes; his pecker standing up like a snake rising to strike. She moved the short distance between them, took hold of his long, tangled hair and yanked him to her, pressed her mouth against his, and even from where we stood, that kiss sounded like someone pulling their foot out of a deep mud puddle.

"That son-of-a-bitch," said the flame-headed guy, who I would later learn was called Red.

The Big Guy picked her up with one arm, leaped off the limb, grabbed another limb with his free hand, swung them up into the cover of a thick-leafed tree, and they were gone. Let me add as an aside, swinging from limb to limb with one hand while holding a very fine and sturdy female is not a feat that anyone else I know of, other than The Big Guy, could accomplish.

I took off.

The men were so shocked to see what had happened, that they didn't know if they should yell or turn in a circle or draw pictures in the dirt. By the time they looked for me, I was across the clearing and into the trees.

[7]

I caught up with The Big Guy and The Woman about nightfall. The Woman had removed her coverings; she was as naked as The Big Guy. There were streaks of blood where the great winged beast had grabbed her, and that attack would leave a scar on her shoulder, three slash marks. The two of them were in the cup of a big limb that had been struck by lightning and hollowed out by it. There were soft leaves laid out in the cup, and they were resting on top of them. What they were doing wouldn't pass for anything other than what it was; I'll use a more common English phrase. They were fucking like there was no tomorrow.

They were so at it I didn't even announce that I had shown up, though The Big Guy could smell me. As he did his business, her screaming and him grunting, he waved a hand at me that let me know to keep my distance. I did. But I watched. Carefully. I had never seen such goings on. Usually, in the jungle, we jump it and do it and get on with looking for something to eat.

This was different. He moved her in different positions, and she let him, and it was well midday when they quit cooing and fell asleep in the cup of the limb. I sat around for awhile, then went out and found some fruit to eat. I brought some of it back with me.

They ate the fruit I brought, and then they went back at it. I think somewhere in all this The Woman realized from the way The Big Guy and myself interacted, that I wasn't a pet. I didn't know that's what she was thinking at the time, but I can look back on events now with acquired knowledge. I think it's a little different knowing the family dog is watching you go at it, but once you realize that what you thought was a pet is a best friend having secondary thrills, that changes thing.

When that realization settled down on her, she got downright prudish. I was surprised The Big Guy didn't just make her do what he wanted, because as I said, we were primitive, but he didn't. He seemed hurt by her reaction. He pouted. He made hooting noises, clicking noises, and screaming noises for complaint. For her complaint, she slapped him so hard it knocked him off the limb.

He grabbed another. Climbed rapidly back up. His face had a red mark in the shape of her fingers on it. I thought this was it. Now we were going to kill her and eat her. But no, that didn't happen.

When he was back up there with her, he hung his head and whimpered. She looked at him for a long moment, her face softened, and she took him into her arms and held him, looking at me over his shoulder with a glare that was nearly strong enough to kill the fleas in my fur.

Me, I went hunting.

[8]

Now, I could go into a blow by blow recreation of what happened next, but frankly, that part is not all that interesting. Simply put, The Woman, having covered herself in her coverings again, took the The Big Guy back to the camp with her, or to be more precise, nearby, and I went along with them. She had somehow developed a way of making the The Big Guy understand what she wanted, mostly with hand motions, and I believe this was possible because they were so naturally attracted to one another.

Anyway, she went into camp and did some talking while we watched from hiding, tucked back in the bush. There was some yelling from the flame-headed man, who had tried to shoot The Big Guy, and there was a lot of conversation from the others, but finally she came to collect us and led us into camp. The Big Guy went without hesitation, being so caught up in The Woman's spell. I on the other hand was nervous. The flamed-headed man, Red, who had tried to shoot The Big Guy, was eyeing us and then looking toward his rifle which was stacked against a tree nearby. He wanted that thing as bad as a worm wants a corpse.

We walked for a ways with them for no other reason than we were invited and wanted to, and in time, just before the sun melted down into the jungle and the ground, we came to a long, dark thing that looked like some kind of giant vegetable. It bobbed in the air on ropes. It was not high off the ground, and underneath it was a kind of box-shape with what to me then looked like eyes that went all the way around, but were in fact glass housed in the frames of a cabin. I know now that it was a zeppelin. There was wooden ramp that led up from the ground to the opening of the cabin. We were easily convinced to go up that ramp and inside, and then the ramp came up and became our door, and we were closed in.

There wasn't any panic. We had not been forced, and in fact, it was something we wanted to do. For uncivilized wild men, we proved to be putty in the hands of the woman. A smile and a laugh and everyone was inside, and the ropes that were looped through metal pegs on the ground were let loose with a crank and a groan of machinery, and we were aloft. We rose quickly and smoothly, into the mist that covered our world, and then we lifted up through that roof of mist into clearer air. Up there I saw a great winged lizard flying. I never knew they came this high, because I never knew how high was high. It flapped its wings and the crew of the zeppelin oohed and ahhed, and on we went, high and then wide, over the tops of the slick walls that contained our world. We stood by the glass and watched as that world moved away from us and the world below turned blue. It was water, but we had never seen so much water. It went on forever, and we sailed across it, rising higher and higher, moving quickly away from our home.

We were in a way captured specimens, but we didn't know it. The old bearded man was ecstatic. I don't know what he truly thought about his daughter's escapades with The Big Guy, not what he was thinking down inside of him, but he seemed fine with it. I didn't think about that then, of course, because as I said, our ideas about what is proper and improper varied considerably from those of the civilized, of which I am now one, but later I would think on it and decide either the old man was very progressive about such matters, or the idea that his daughter had lured in such unique specimens as The Big Guy and myself surpassed any sort of fatherly propriety he may have possessed. At this late date, and it's still only a guess, I am going with the former view instead of the latter.

So there we were, as stunned as if we had been run over by a water buffalo, looking out the window glass of the cabin as the zeppelin rose up and our world became a dark line in the distance capped with fog, resting there in the great blue water in such a way it seemed the sky had been turned upside down and the dark line of our home was a wound in the fallen sky, blanketed by a cloud.

Inside the cabin there was plenty of space. There was a man in a funny hat standing at the wheel beside the captain, a position I learned of later. The captain's name was Zeppner and he worked for Dr. Rice. There were many other crew members, and there were a number of jobs they did. During the time we were aloft, and that was a goodly time, we would find out that the cabin branched out through a door and there was a place where the cook prepared meals and there was a mess, and there were rooms off of it. One of these rooms we shared with The Woman's father, so perhaps his propriety was wider and deeper than I would think, but it may have been merely a polite custom to separate a man without clothes from his daughter, as well as myself. I think it took a few days for them to decide if I was man or animal. I think the final decision was somewhere in-between.

Dr. Rice was not only our roommate, but a man who began teaching us his language and certain customs long before we reached the shores of Japanese-America, and later European-America. We also made friends with the navigator, Bowen Tyler, of which adventure books have also been written, most of them exaggerated lies, and by the same liar who told the stories about The Big Guy and me, though I will admit he got a few things right, if only perhaps by accident.

Anyway, we were given pants, and I took to mine right away, but had to learn about unfastening them and pulling them down when the urge to let loose with inner workings arrived on the wings of nature. I ruined several pairs of pants before I got that right. The Big Guy wore the pants all right, but he didn't like shirts at all and wouldn't wear them for the longest time, and he never did really take to shoes. I liked them, but there were none in the zeppelin that would fit me.

The days passed. On we went. Over mountains and jungles and more water and land dotted in the water, and finally back to more water again; a blueness that appeared to stretch out until it linked up with the sky.

●●●

As I was saying, during the trip I began to learn words of English, which was the main language spoken by Americans, even the Japanese side. I learned that at one time there had been a war, and one side of this huge country we were going to had been taken over by the Japanese, but in time they united. Still, the West Coast was called Japanese-America, the East, European-America. On the zeppelin there were also a few Japanese. During the trip I began to see the differences in them and the others. Before, when I had seen them as a group, except for the hair on the faces of some, I hadn't realized they were different; to me they were all the same, people like The Big Guy, but smaller. I learned to say "please" and "thank you" and "pass the peas," and for a long time I thought all food was called peas. I also learned words like "fuck" and "shit," "damn, hell, goddamn" and the like, but it took me some time to learn how to use them in properly in polite conversation.

So we flew and we flew and The Big Guy and The Woman were often together, much to the disappoint-ment of flame-head, or Red as he was known. You could see the anger coming out of him. He looked easily as sav-age as the wildest things me and The Big Guy had ever encountered. But from previous experience, Red knew going up against The Big Guy would lead to him losing a few parts, so with steam almost blowing out of his ears, he held his temper and watched them stand beside each other, look at each other and smile and say nothing, and sometimes they held hands, and I am sure there were times in secret places that they did more than that.

When we were near our destination, New York, they gave me and The Big Guy some fresh pants and shirts, but neither of us wore shoes, The Big Guy because he wouldn't, and me because as I said, none fit. We didn't really need them. The bottoms of our feet were hard as wood and we could step on thorns and glass and not have them penetrate. They also gave The Big Guy a tie for some reason, and he used it to bind back his long hair, which The Woman had trimmed considerably, after combing out burrs and thorns and minor wildlife. She even gave me a good brushing, and I liked it so much, that I did it myself several times a day. I liked the way it made my hair shine.

We had never seen buildings before, and in the wheel-house, looking out of the glass, those buildings looked like odd mountains at first. When the craft docked at what they called the Empire State building, I was almost beside myself. So was The Big Guy.

"Son-of-a-bitch," I said.

"Very good," said Dr. Rice. "That is a proper usage of the word, if not the literal meaning."

"Thank you," I said. I tell you, right then I felt like one sophisticated motherfucker, that motherfucker word being something I learned later.

[9]

Me and The Big Guy were all the rage. We were paraded about like circus animals and asked to do all manner of things. The Big Guy bent metal bars and broke ropes with his chest and climbed up the sides of buildings like a big bug. I couldn't bend the bars, but I could break a lot of ropes and climbing was my middle name. It's actually Uchugucdagarmindoonie, but that's not important. Besides, looking at it now, spelled out, I have to say that is only a close approximation, so we just won't worry about it.

Anyway, we were taken here and there, poked and probed by doctors, and on one occasion a greased finger was jammed up my butt, which resulted in an unexpected thrill. We were needled and measured, asked to run and be timed, asked to climb and be timed. They watched us eat, watched us talk English in our peculiar way. They listened to the old language, the language we knew, and they made notes. They were amazed at how hard the bottoms of our feet were. They were equally amazed at the overall condition of The Big Guy's muscles and teeth. Mine they were equally impressed with, especially my more pronounced canines.

Next thing that happened was we had lessons in manners.

We learned to sit in chairs, sleep in beds, take baths, eat with utensils instead of our fingers, and to take our time about meals. We had to grasp the idea that no one or anything was going to spring on us from under the table or out of a closet and wrestle us all over the room for our food. This was one of the more difficult changes for the two of us, due to us having come from a world where when food was found you wolfed it down to make sure you got to keep it, or to make sure it didn't bite you back; and you eyed everyone and everything around you suspiciously, lest they be reaching for your chow. They soon learned how engrained this was when one of our table companions reached casually for the salt shaker, only to end up with The Big Guy grabbing him by the head and flinging him across the room. He thought the man was going for his baked trout.

To make sure the man understood The Big Guy's dominance, The Big Guy not only finished his own trout as quick as a wild pig snuffing up a grub worm, he ate the man's trout as well, jumped to the middle of the table and started stuffing the dessert (a cake) into his mouth as fast as he could reach with both hands.

Instinct and experience taking over, me knowing how much that big bastard eat, and having gone to bed hungry because him in the past, I too leaped onto the table and started snatching, which led to a mild grapple between the two of us which resulted in my being bit on the shoulder and having a handful of cake stuffed in my ear and a random carrot shoved in my nose.

What could you expect? We were savages. But we did learn some civilized activities. We learned to drink, and I learned to smoke (The Big Guy never took to it), and I learned to chase women. The Big Guy had his woman, and he stuck with her. They had even taken to living in the same hotel room. But me, well, I was a goddamn celebrity, and I had groupies. They all wanted to hump Mr. Hairy. I rush in here to say this was a title given to me by the newspapers for a time (fortunately it didn't stick) and one I never embraced. But the women embraced me, and I came to find them attractive, not just usable. I began to like to wear suit coats and ties, well-creased pants, and shoes, though I always had to cut them open at the front so my toes had room. In short time I took to wearing open toed house shoes. It became all the rage with the kids. The sale of house shoes went up, and pretty soon I was modeling them in magazines, wearing a tux with those fuzzy shoes on my feet. They pretty much became my trademark. I was loved by the young and the sophisticated, disliked by parents and the clergy.

I went to fine restaurants and learned to order wine. I will tell you truthfully, I took to the life. It beat climbing trees to flee wild animals. It beat looking for fruit and eating bugs and worms, or chasing down some swift animal with a stick or a rock. I liked the nice rooms in the great hotel where we were kept. I liked the bed with its clean, cool sheets better than I liked a leafy nest on the ground or the crook of a tree. I liked room service. I liked the women who slept with me; or rather I liked what we did. No particular woman ever stayed with me more than a day and a night. I wouldn't let them, even though there were many who wanted to. There were just too many opportunities, too many offers, and I took advantage of it.

I was drinking until late, smoking cigars and sometimes a pipe. I was learning to tell jokes and talk in a sophisticated manner. I knew how to get my arm around women's shoulders without being awkward, and I had gained quite a reputation in the tabloids as a ladies' man.

And I was becoming famous and admired. Maybe not as much as The Big Guy, but it was a new experience for me. Back home I was, to sum it up in crass and modern terms, just another monkey, because even though he was different from the rest of us—perhaps because he was—he was always held in higher esteem than me. At home, I was just like everyone else there, but in New York, I was special.

In time this fame led to The Big Guy and myself becoming movie stars.

At least for awhile.

[10]

You went to the movies, you saw all manner of things in the newsreels about us. Saw us climbing trees and doing this or that, The Big Guy bending those iron bars and so on, and it was only natural that Japanese-America and Hollywood came calling.

This was sometime after we had been in New York, and we had learned the language reasonably quick and reasonably well; well enough to do simple interviews.

We flew out there in a smaller zeppelin than the one that had brought us to New York. We landed in a field near the ocean. There were reporters and cameras everywhere. We did interview after interview.

"What do you think about our world?" a reporter asked The Big Guy.

"Busy," he said.

"What do you think about our women?"

"I think about The Woman all the time." He called her that, same as me, but they thought he just didn't know how to say women, and so it was reported that he thought about women all the time. This led to women throwing themselves at him in even greater abundance than before. He ignored them even when a fine doll would toss a pair of underpants in his face, or a room key. It wasn't a moral code that kept him from humping them; it was a sincere love for The Woman, who was back in New York teaching anthropology at a university. Me, I was damn near screwing anything except a hole in the ground. But The Big Guy was truly lonely. While we were out there in moving picture land, sometimes he would go out on the hotel veranda and look up at the moon and howl. Sometimes he whacked off. This was a behavior he had been taught to modify in public; out there he just put his hand in his pocket, but he knew I didn't care. That was just SOP for us back home. While he was at it I read a magazine and drank a cup of coffee. This was the kind of activity that our handlers were always afraid of. Fearing we might go primitive during an interview, and frankly, it was a legitimate concern. It was hard to figure things out.

"Where is your home?" reporters asked.

The Big Guy shook his head. They thought he was being coy, but it was an honest answer. We had no way of knowing where our home was, not after that long flight. And in fact, old Dr. Rice wasn't telling either. The crew had been sworn to secrecy due to scientific research and Rice wanting to keep the place unknown due to fear that it would soon be swamped by explorers and curiosity seekers. There was also this: No one except him and the navigator truly understood its locale, and to be honest, most people thought it was a big publicity hoax, that The Big Guy was some Hollywood muscle man, and that I was a fellow with a disease that caused me to grow hair all over my body. We never did shake that whole hoax business. It still follows us around.

Anyway, there were all these interviews, and then we were given lines to learn and deliver. We made two pictures.

We got a few calls from the desk about the howling, but that didn't stop him, and being the celebrity he was, no one wanted to really corner him on it. Besides, he had a look in his eye when approached about such behavior that made you feel as if he were just looking for a reason to reach down your throat, grab your asshole, and pull it up through the big middle of you.

As for the pictures we made while we were out there, they were terrible. We were the real deal, but we couldn't act our way out of a paper bag with a pair of scissors. We didn't really understand what acting actually was. They had these scenes where "natives" would attack, and me and The Big Guy would just actually beat the hell out of them. We had to really work to play at it; play of that sort wasn't in our nature. You showed up with a weapon, even if it turned out to be made of balsa wood, and waved it around, it triggered our defense mechanisms. We broke up a lot of stuntmen.

Also, on the second picture there was an unpleasant incident with a lion. There were lions on the lost world where we lived, but they were lions without manes, and they were much bigger. Our greatest fear in the form of jungle cats on our world wasn't actually the lion. It's what are called by those who study bones, saber-toothed tigers, thought to be extinct. Maybe everywhere else, but not where we are from. And the dinosaurs in those two pictures we made—stop motion and men in suits—were just plain silly, and didn't look anything like the real deal. But damn it, there I go again. Distracted. I was talking about the movie we were in and how a supposedly tame lion on the set went wonky and jumped on the girl who was playing The Woman (we portrayed ourselves, The Woman did not), and The Big Guy strangled it as easily as a kitten. He was a hero up to that point, because there had been considerable panic on set, but when the cat was dead, The Big Guy jerked off the loin cloth they had given him to wear (we, of course, never wore any), yanked it up by the tail, and diddled it in its dead ass right there, then threw it on the ground, put his foot on its neck, lifted his head and howled. This was his way of showing dominance, acceptable behavior where we came from when there had been a life and death struggle. It wasn't necessary for an antelope, and some of the creatures were a bit too large for this act of dominance, but, still, it was considered just part of our way of life when it came to big dangerous predators. It was a way of showing who was boss. This, in civilization, however, was looked down upon even more than whacking off in public.

Observers on the set took this out of context and thought it to be deviant. The set was abandoned for the day and no one would talk to The Big Guy for awhile, and certainly wouldn't turn their backs on him. Me, I was proud of him. That said, the rest of the shoot was a nervous event.

Anyway, Hollywood is Hollywood, and there was money in the picture and money in us, and the public was waiting, even though the first picture had gotten the worst reviews of any film ever made. What counted was it had been a big financial hit. The director, who was devastated, retired from the movies and went into advertising.

That was the end of our movie career as actors, even though that lion screwing incident didn't end up in the last picture we made. It had been filmed, but that part of the movie was removed, though there was gossip about it from some of those on the set who had seen it. That gossip grew into a larger crowd that claimed to have witnessed the incident. If all of those who claimed to have seen it had, then the movie set that day would have been packed with a thousand people for a scene that only contained The Big Guy, the actress, me, and the lion, a skeleton crew, and a mess of false tree and brush props.

We went back to New York.

The rumors didn't kill our popularity. Not at first, (we'll come back to that) because there wasn't any actual revealed evidence it ever happened; it seemed so bizarre to Americans on either coast, and in the middle of the country, it was mostly thought of as an anecdotal story.

As for future pictures, they hired an actor to play The Big Guy, and got that damn chimpanzee to play me. When the actor pretended to kill a lion, or some beast in the movies, he put his foot on it and howled. No diddling allowed. The chest beating and the howling were correct, but the other thing missing just sort of dulled the situation. But, from an acting standpoint, our replacements were better and the movies still made money and made us even more famous. They made eight movies back to back about us with that actor pair, all of them major hits. There were lunch boxes and thermoses and tee-shirts and bread and milk products with our pictures on it. I still have a lunch box with a thermos, and for the right price, I'm willing to let it go.

By the time the first four pictures came out, the two with us, and the first two with the other guy and that chimp, we were rich as fresh-whipped butter. Something I learned about my adopted land was that if you had money, and if you were making other people money, you could diddle a lion at high noon in Times Square and most everyone would get over it, even the kids, as long as you didn't have the actual film to prove it, of course.

[11]

Now the odd thing was, in a short time, the actors who played us became better known than us, and many people forgot that we were the real ape-men of the jungle—me being a little closer anthropologically in that department. We were old news, and that damn chimpanzee, even after he quit playing the part, as I said earlier, got special attention each year on his birthday. Cake and candles. We didn't get that. But, we did get royalty checks, so there was a trade off. In that way I prefer what we got to what that damn ape got, though I still bristle at his popularity, and that now, so many years later, me and The Big Guy are mostly forgotten and the memory of the actor and that chimpanzee have taken our place.

The whole thing began to get to The Big Guy. The whole thing being the world we were living in. He just couldn't understand it. He discovered alcohol, and he could drink a lot of it. That stuff was to him like nectar to a bee. He became bourbon's bitch. He was so drunk most of the time The Woman began knocking on my door late at night to ask if she could sleep on my couch while he raved and cursed in our ape-man tongue. Sometimes when he drank up all the hotel room booze, he climbed out the window, down the side of the building and into the street, and away he would go, dressed in clothes but not wearing any shoes.

He drank his way from one end of town to the other. One night he climbed over the walls of the zoo, bent bars, and let all manner of wild animals out. It was kept out of the papers, but a couple of tigers ate a bum and two orphans who were sleeping under a bridge. They weren't tax payers, so it was easy to sweep under the rug. Way The Big Guy saw it animals were supposed to be free. They could kill or be killed in a wild world situation, but cages, that bugged him, bugged him big time. In a way, I think he came to see the hotel, and even the whole of New York, as nothing more than a kind of cage that held him back from where he wanted to be, from the life he wanted to live.

Me, I was digging it. I got so I kept my body hair trimmed close, dressed nice, wore a monocle and a top hat and very nice suits. I took to going to jazz clubs, learned to play the bongos, smoked big cigars. I liked having an evening martini, wearing my bathrobe and slippers. I even did a little record album with a couple of those cool jazz cats; one of them on bass, one on sax, and me beating the skins. I got so I could lay down quite a few French phrases and a smidgeon of Italian. And

KenLaager

there was another thing. Me and The Woman, all those nights she slept on my couch... Well, we got close. We talked about The Big Guy. We worried about him. We cried over him. We hugged each other in sympathy. In short time I was laying the pipe to her like I was running a gas line from here to Cuba. We didn't mean for it to happen. It just did. The Woman told me that before I took her to bed, she and The Big Guy hadn't had sex in three months. He had found a substitute for sex: whisky, beer, wine and vodka, as well as his favorite, bourbon, and sometimes a little rubbing alcohol taken from the medicine cabinet over the sink. He had even been known to drink hair oil. He had the itch bad.

He had also became a bigger spectacle and public disgrace. Shedding his clothes. Running naked through the streets. Climbing the Empire State building, all the way to the top where the zeppelin dock was. Swimming in public fountains, pulling one of the stone lions down from its pedestal at the New York Public library. Just got hold of it and yanked that big sucker off its pedestal and broke it to pieces. He even swam out to the Statue of Liberty. Can you imagine that. I can't swim at all, but he swam all the way out there, climbed it because he can, had a hot dog from a vendor, and swam back; all of this done without a stitch on, just like in the old days.

Here's something I'm really ashamed of. I began to be embarrassed of The Big Guy. My best friend. My brother. We had done a lot of things together in the old days that were no worse than the things he was doing

now, in the new days. Bless me, but I was starting to shake my head and cluck my tongue. To be honest, I really enjoyed banging his old lady. That doesn't mean I quit feeling for him. Late at night, holding The Woman in my arms, after I had drunk my martini and had my fun with her, I would think. Shit, that's tough on the old boy, me with his girl and him not knowing, and me not telling, and her not telling. But that didn't change me. I stayed the same. That sweet, warm, woman and the cool, clean sheets, and the toilet where you could sit and read without fear of being attacked by some manner of beast, were much too satisfying to want to give up.

●●●

Now, I told you about that red-headed man who had loved The Woman and thought he was going to end up with her, but after The Big Guy came along, he might as well have been the balls on a brass monkey. She had no interest in him, and now, of course, her interest was in me. Or at least it was to some degree. I won't kid you. Sometimes I would awake and find her missing from my arms. She would be sitting in a chair by the great open window that led out on the veranda that overlooked the light-winking city, naked, her blonde hair dangling, the moonlight nestled in those scars on her shoulders, her breasts spear-tipped from the cool air, and I could tell she was thinking about The Big Guy. Somewhere, maybe he was thinking about her. It was hard to say. He seldom came back to the hotel anymore, which is why he didn't miss her from his bed. He slept atop buildings, or in the park, or on a bench, usually clutching a bottle of booze in a brown paper bag. I had brought him home many a time in that condition, until I finally gave it up. Nothing changed him. I even talked to him about The Woman. I didn't mention that me and her were doing the nasty—though I would never have thought of it that way in the wild—but it didn't change him. I like to think had he come to his senses that me and The Woman could have shook hands and just been friends and they could have gone back together, the way it was supposed to be. But he didn't change. The alcohol had numbed his senses—a lot. But he knew something wasn't right between me and him and him and her, even though he didn't know it was what it was; he trusted us both too much for that. I could tell the way his beautiful eyes rested on me that he knew our friendship was washing up on the rocks, yet I'm certain he didn't actually suspect me of such treachery as taking from him the thing he loved the most in the world, The Woman; well, that and his freedom, his desire to go back to the way things were. I think he might have been willing to share her, and maybe The Woman would even have gone for that—she was progressive, but it just didn't occur to him that she needed him in her arms and in her bed. Like I said, that ole John Barley Corn had him by the nuts.

I have wandered again. I was telling you about the red-headed man.

You see, Red, as most people called him, never gave up on The Woman. One look at her and you would know why. She was a stunner, as I have said, but there was something else about her. It was—and this is going to sound like a cheap romance story—her soul; it reached out to you and embraced you. Corny as that sounds, I don't know any other way to describe it. She was something. For Red, though, I think it was that he thought he had her locked down, and when the lock broke, he couldn't accept it. Maybe if he had been the one to break it off he would have been fine. He was that kind of guy. Everything on his terms. Only thing was, The Big Guy wasn't interested in terms. Red knew that any interference there would just lead to him having his head pulled off like a grape plucked from the vine, so he bided his time. When things fell apart for The Big Guy and The Woman, he was waiting, and I am certain (without actual evidence, I admit) he was the one who finally leaked the lion diddling event to the public. We were told at first it was destroyed. Another time were told it existed, but that it was lost, and finally that it was stolen. And then it showed up. I think Red bought it from someone, maybe the director who had gone into advertising. I can't say. But he got his hands on it.

That wasn't what happened first, though. That wasn't the first brick pulled from the pile. There were several. I guess I should have snapped to it, but I admit that I had been for the most part civilized and my instincts were not as sharply honed as they once were. Two or three times I thought I was being followed, and had noticed someone in the streets that I had seen twice earlier that day. New York is a big city, but people cross paths with one another now and again, so I didn't think much of it. It wasn't until The Woman and I had come back from a party, a little liquor-buzzed and hot to trot for the old bed room, when I smelled something. We had just come in through the door, and even though I was a bit drunk, and as I have said, civilized, something kicked in. I got a whiff of someone having been in our hotel room. Not a maid. I knew all their scents, and had had relations with several before me and The Woman took up together, and once or twice when she was out of town. This was the scent of a man with too much cologne. I peeled The Woman off of me, told her to wait, and sniffed about. My sniffing eventually led to a little camera fastened into a light fixture over our bed. Way it was rigged, when you turned on the light it came on and started snapping pictures, and when you turned it off, it still snapped for awhile. That way it had you in full light, and then, because our window always had the big curtains thrown back, and there were lights from the city resting on our bed, we could be easily photographed doing whatever we were doing, and frequently we were doing a lot.

At first, I was elated, thinking I had found the camera before any photos could be taken. Then it occurred to me that the only reason I knew someone had been in the room was the cologne. A strange thought passed through me. What if, with my senses dulled, I had missed somebody having entered our room before, when they weren't wearing cologne? The camera could have taken many photos, and it only had to have its film replaced from time to time, something that could easily be done when we were out of the room. What if there were already photos of us?

I pulled the camera out and showed it to The Woman, who gasped. You see, there was some part of us that played like this was all a momentary fling. That when it came right down to it, all was right with her and The Big Guy, or soon would be, but that camera made us feel otherwise.

"Perhaps it's blackmail," The Woman said.

I nodded, thinking perhaps that was it. I suppose The Big Guy could have had someone do it, to check up on us, but that didn't seem likely. Unlike me, he never learned guile. I learned it when we lived in our lost world, and I had perfected it in civilization. Maybe whoever had set this photographic trap would want money instead of showing it to The Big Guy, but I tell you, right then I had a hunch who it was and what it was about. It came to me like a tick crawling into my arm pit that Red was behind all this, that he had hired someone to follow us, and to plant that camera, and what he wanted wasn't money. He wanted revenge.

[12]

Yeah, I hadn't thought of Red in ages, but right then, down deep in my bones, I knew it was him, and what hit me the hardest was that there was something for him to find, something he could let The Big Guy see so that it harmed his pride and took away the only reason he had allowed himself to be hoodwinked into coming to this world.

The Big Guy trusted us, especially me. We had been brothers since he was a baby. Right at that moment I felt the way I should have felt all along. Like a traitor.

I smashed the camera on the floor.

But you know what? I still went to bed with The Woman.

The next day that lion bumping film was released and seen in private by a number of newspaper men who reported on it. It wasn't seemly for it to be shown to the public, and wasn't, at least at that period in time. But it was written about, and a few stills were published in the rags, and though they weren't explicit, it was clear what was going on. Shots of the dead lion facing us, its tongue lagging out of its mouth, The Big Guy clutching its tail, lifting it into position for... Well, it was obvious. There had been the rumors before, but now there was the film. I told you how it is with money, how it offered lots of insulation. But The Big Guy took a hit with the public. Not that he cared, but that's what happened. Our two movies were removed from circulation, and even to this day they are seldom shown, and only on late night television.

But the day it hit I found out about it in the morning paper. I tried to hide it from The Woman, but too late. She saw it. It made our souls and stomachs sink, and you would think we would just lock our hotel room door and hide. Or maybe at least have the guts to somehow talk to The Big Guy, own up to what we had done, and try to commiserate with him over the news, though that part about the lion probably didn't bother him the way it would others. For him, that was an accepted ritual. And once, it had been for me as well.

As I said, you'd think we'd do that, commiserate with The Big Guy, but we didn't. We took the cowardly way out and tried to make things better for ourselves. We went out for a drive. It's not that we weren't concerned, but we were determined to not let some asshole with a camera ruin our life, and like I said, we were cowards. We drove outside of New York and into the country. There was a nice place there where we could have a picnic. We parked the Packard and rolled our blanket on the ground, set out our picnic basket stuffed with very fine foods, a thermos of good wine, as well as a thermos of Italian coffee. We had paper plates and cups, and we ate and laughed and kissed, trying to make our worries go away, but the truth is they hung over us like a rain cloud even though the sky was clear and beautiful. After awhile we lay back on the blanket, in each other's arms, digested and looked at the sky. I rose up on one elbow to pry off the thermos lid to the coffee, and that's when I saw him.

The Big Guy. He was a pretty good distance away, on a hill covered by trees. In the tallest tree, mostly hidden by leaves, he sat in the fork of a limb and watched us.

I knew then that Red had not only had the camera put in my hotel room, but that most likely shots from that camera had been put in an envelope and somehow slipped to The Big Guy, just as we feared.

The Big Guy knew I saw him. He dropped from the tree, light as a bird, disappeared behind the hill. I expected he would come rushing down that hill to destroy us at any moment, and I didn't intend to put up a fight, not even to protect her.

The Woman had seen him as well. She had tears in her eyes.

We waited.

He didn't come rushing down after us.

I heard a car start up behind the trees and race away.

I could tell by the sound of the engine that it was his Buick, the one he hardly drove and really shouldn't drive at all. The Big Guy could do many things, but he never really learned to drive too well. He was always being pulled out of ditches and having to pay other drivers for banging up their cars. But he had been smart enough to ease up behind that hill silently, get out and climb that tree. Now he didn't care. About anything was my guess.

You want to know what hurt me the most right then? That he didn't even have the courtesy to kill us.

[13]

After that, it was over with me and The Woman.

I decided what I had to do was confront The Big Guy, lay it all out and hope he didn't yank off my leg and beat me to death with it. I desperately wanted to make amends. But he wasn't in his room. I couldn't find him. I walked all over the city, took taxies and trains to his favorite haunts, but nothing. I must have gone through every bar in New York City that next week, but I couldn't find him. The Woman had gone back to their room to wait for him, to hope for the best. But he hardly ever went there. Up until the other day he didn't seem too concerned about where she was, or even where he was. But I could imagine him seeing those photos, my hairy ass on top of her, doing the deed. It made me sick to my stomach.

I didn't really want to see her again, but I went to her and told her that I had searched everywhere, and had pretty much given up.

JOE R. LANSDALE

"Any ideas?" I said.

"The hospitals," she said.

"Beg pardon?" I said.

"He may have been injured. You know how he drove. He may be in the hospital."

Well, that got me to a phone right away. I started checking around, and sure enough, we found him. Downtown, right near the hotel, in a hospital room. Two broken legs, a broken arm, smashed ribs, and a concussion. He'd been there all week, under an assumed name. He hadn't done that, a doctor had, knowing there was so much publicity afoot concerning the film of him and the lion. It was a damn noble thing to do, I thought, though later I found out he sold his story to one of the cheap-ass rags, and for not that much money, I might add.

When I finally saw the police report a couple days later, it was revealed that he had driven down a hill on his way back into the city at top speed. A motorist behind him said, "He just yanked the wheel to the left, off the curve, and over the side of the big hill. The car flew like a plane. Was in the air all the way down until it hit a brick fence around a sheep farm. Tore that fence down, and one of the sheep died of a heart attack. It didn't do the car any good either."

The Good Samaritan drove to a nearby farmhouse, called the law and an ambulance. That's how The Big Guy ended up in the hospital, wrapped up like a mummy, his legs lifted in traction. The nurse told us that three days later he came around, but they couldn't get him to

[74]

eat or drink. He seemed to want to die. They finally used heavy drugs to put him completely out, help him deal with the pain. I thought, yeah, the pain. The only thing he was pained about was seeing me and The Woman together like that. Broken bones were nothing to him.

After he was knocked out, they kept him that way, ended up hooking him to a feeder tube and an IV. We went and sat by his bed, and when they tried to make us leave because visiting hours were over, we wouldn't. They finally gave up and let us stay. The Woman held the hand of the arm that wasn't broken, and I just sat in my chair with tears in my eyes and looked at him.

The Good Life had ruined all three of us.

•••

One morning, The Big Guy still on the mend, The Woman at the hospital with him, I went to see Dr. Rice, and laid out my plan. I said, "Doctor, The Big Guy, he's not doing so well. Civilization hasn't taken with him like it has with me. He needs to go back."

The old man nodded. He said, "And back he shall go."

Remember, the location of our home on the world in the mist had been kept secret by Dr. Rice, and a couple of other individuals, including the navigator, one Bowen Tyler. Red and a few others had been on that trek, but they were all trusted individuals, except for Red, who had been there due to the fact he was then The Woman's boyfriend, and a known hunter and tracker. He could find his way through the jungle, but no one thought he knew the path to our world across that vast ocean, so any knowledge he had wasn't a great concern. And at that moment, no one knew where he was. Nothing had actually been proven to suggest he had been the one behind the lion-fucking leak, or for that matter, the camera in our room, so there was nothing to do legally, though it was in the back of my mind to give him a visit if I got the chance so that what was inside of him could be found painting the walls of his abode, wherever that was.

Remember too, for the most part we were considered the perpetrators of a hoax to sell tickets in Hollywood, so that gave us a bit of insulation, and was part of the reason crew members had been silent in regards to discussing where we had come from. To talk about us in a positive way was the same as telling their neighbors they had seen the Abominable Snowman in their backyard having a cookout on their barbecue grill with a nude female leprechaun.

We made plans. The Big Guy was going back, and I had a pretty good idea that The Woman was going back with him. While The Big Guy was on the mend, it was pretty obvious that he and The Woman had found their connection again. It was also clear, though I had betrayed my friend, he had forgiven me. He said so. I suppose that he actually had always known. The photographs that he found in his hotel room were just the icing on the cake. In fact, it was a rare thing for him to go back to that room, but he had, and they had been waiting. Yeah, the photos were the icing, but he had known about the cake for a long time, or certainly suspected it was baking in the oven. I think he forgave me because he understood. The Woman was a force unto herself, and he felt he had been as responsible for our situation as much as we had. I didn't agree. Friendship should have stood steadfast, woman or no woman. But, then we come back to that part about it being her, and if you've ever seen her, you would understand. I don't mean photos of her. Oh, she looks fine, no doubt. But if you had actually ever SEEN her in person, you would know. No other woman could hold your fancy after that. She was a goddamn goddess.

In our old world The Big Guy would be away from alcohol and things he didn't truly understand. He would be with The Woman. He could speak the old language and live the old ways. And me, I could come back to New York City where I truly belonged, among the civilized. I didn't find the savage life all that appealing anymore. It was different when it was all that I knew, but I liked my winter heat and summer air-conditioning and no flying beasts and saber-toothed cats. I liked what my money from the movie royalties could buy. It was my intent when I came back to get a college degree. I thought I might teach anthropology. Lots of college girls around, nice cushy job, retirement, and all that shit. It beat working, which with the money I had coming in from the films I wouldn't have to do for a long time to come; but truth be told, it wouldn't last forever. Already the checks were slightly smaller. It was a matter of time, and I had to plan for the future, and I didn't have any plans where I would be out in the jungle with my ass hanging out in the wind, glancing over my shoulder for predators.

It took about two more months for them to get the zeppelin refurbished and for Dr. Rice to get the old navigator on the task. Turned out Bowen Tyler had retired from navigating air flights and was living in Greenwich in England (the half that belonged to Germany; he was there on a visa), and he was teaching at a small college in the area. He really didn't want to go back into the air, but, as he was one of the few who knew how to get to our little lost world, we told him it was necessary, and he kindly agreed. We also knew we could trust Tyler, as he had refused to give the location of our world these last few years, though he was constantly asked. He had written about it, but never in any detail. His work was a fictional account, and I will be quick to add it is very fictional and has little to do with the truth. He got the part right about how savage the place was, about the creatures that lived there, but the rest of it, about evolutionary pools and submarines, and so on, that was just pulp magazine junk. Another reason we have been marked down to nothing more than a hoax. But hell, that's all right with me.

Bottom line is it all got planned. The Big Guy healed up good as new. That's how he was. He could mend quickly, and considering how many injuries he had from that car crash, it was amazing. The doctors who worked on him were astonished. One of them, a nice man named Dr. Cupp, told me that there was something different about The Big Guy's insides, that it appeared as if everything was unique about his body. That would have been the injection he received from his parents, but I didn't say that, though I had done a bit of research on the matter, and figured that the drug he had been given not only gave him long life, but made him capable of healing rapidly and perfectly. He could be hurt, and he could die, but because of that drug, he had advantages over you and me.

Now, if you are paying attention, I bet you are thinking about now what I was thinking about then, and it was simply that The Woman didn't have that serum in her blood. What happened when she aged, and he did not? It was an ugly thing to think about. I decided for the time being to be silent.

[14]

On an early morning with the copper sun edging into the city, we launched off from atop the Empire State Building and into the rising light. No cars and no people visible; the city had not truly awakened yet. It was so quiet up there you could have heard a gnat fart. As we rose, a flock of white birds flew before us, and I took that as a good omen.

Let me tell you what I know now.

Omens are for shit.

•••

The zeppelin had been worked on and retooled. It was larger, but swifter. It had less of a crew than when we first rode in it, and it was, according to Dr. Rice, a trustworthy crew. The zeppelin was stuffed with food and water and even a few barrels of beer and a stocked wine closet. There were two biplanes as well, one on either side of the wheelhouse. They were held by clamps that could be worked from the open cockpit of the planes to release them. There were a number of guns on board. There were some trade goods. The Big Guy had tried to discourage this aspect, trading with the natives, as he had seen what civilization could do to us (I, as I said, liked it. He didn't), but Dr. Rice was determined that if he was going to lose The Big Guy and his daughter as well— for he knew the score and wanted her to be happy—he demanded an opportunity to work among my people, explore the island, bring back native items, write about his experiences, but not give away its location.

By the time we were four days out I couldn't shake a feeling of doom. Perhaps it was because I knew I was not staying with The Big Guy, and The Woman was going with him, and I was going back to civilization. Fact was, I had already started to crave it, yet, still I hated to leave them. I loved them both.

On the fifth morning the sky darkened. It began to rain and the zeppelin began to jump. I was airsick until late afternoon when the darkness split and the sunlight sliced in and the rain died out. I went to the huge storage room for some bicarbonate of soda to settle my stomach, and while there I saw that some of the food goods had been broken into. A lid on a crate near the back had been lifted and replaced awkwardly, and a wax paper container of crackers was missing from the box. I also noticed that the tins of sardines had been disturbed, many of them strewn about on the floor. I didn't think much of this at the time, as it seemed to me that it was likely one of the crew members that had broken into the goods; far as I was concerned they were welcome to it. I found the bicarbonate of soda, and on my way out I sniffed the air, recognized human urine. Some years back I would have thought nothing of someone pissing wherever they wanted, whenever they wanted, but now this bothered me. Had it only been a bit of the food, I could have stood that, but pissing on the floor? I had become too sophisticated for that.

Angrily, I straightened the askew wine rack on my way out by pushing it with my shoulder, not giving much thought to it being out of place, and determined I would bring these doings to the attention of Dr. Rice. By the time I left the storage room and went to my cabin to put the bicarbonate of soda in a water glass, my anger had subsided. I even considered that The Big Guy might have done it. Gone down there and to get some food and mark his spot. He was still a savage. Years back, I could have sniffed that urine and known who it belonged to, but now my nose was cultured, and all I knew was someone had taken a leak in the storage room. I decided to forget it. I was beginning to be as fussy as an old lady, and I was a little ashamed of myself.

For the next few days the weather was fair. We came to a place in the ocean where a huge mist hung in the air like a veil. A bit of excitement stirred within me then, for this was the world from which I had come, a huge island, or continent—I actually have no idea how large our world really is—clothed in fog produced by the volcanic humidity that warmed our lost world. And even though I liked New York City, I did suffer more than a bit of nostalgia at that moment.

The zeppelin dipped into the mist; everything was a white cloud. Then the zeppelin dropped down even more and the mist thinned. Below there were high, slick, flat gray walls of rock that rose up to incredible heights. As we slipped over the top of that wall there were more clouds. We descended into them slowly. They broke, and what we saw then was mine and The Big Guy's fine green world. Windows were opened on the sides of the wheelhouse, allowing the warmer outside air to stir about. Great leathery lizards flew about, and for a moment there was some consternation that one of them might attack our ship, but we glided down, easy, unmolested. There was a gap in the forest, a savanna, and we coasted toward it. As we did, we saw a herd of large, feathered lizards running on their hind legs, their heads leaning forward as if to show the way. We slowed to observe them continue their path until they were out of sight, then we stopped hovering and headed in for a landing.

Instantly, things went wrong.

●●●

I have thought about this a lot, and I don't know that I have an exact answer, but I have a strong speculation. At first I thought it was just because he had hidden so long, waited so long, was so goddamn angry, he couldn't wait anymore. Instead of waiting until we landed, he came out of hiding and rampaged into the wheelhouse where everyone on board had gathered. He was carrying a revolver. He looked crazy. His red hair was standing up on his head like a blaze of fire. His face was near red as his hair. His eyes were wide and there was saliva drooling from the corners of his mouth. He looked like a man about to blow a major hose, and in that moment I knew his hatred of The Big Guy had driven him somewhat mad.

You have probably guessed by now that Red had stowed on board, and that he had been the one who had been at the crackers and sardines, pissed all over he place, and when I pushed that wine rack back in place, all I did was help conceal him better, hiding back there behind it, probably on some makeshift bed. I curse myself for not being observant enough to have noticed.

Red came storming into the wheelhouse carrying a revolver, calling The Big Guy a goddamn whoremonger, and calling The Woman a whore and a shit poke, and to top it off, he called me a fucking, chattering monkey. I will admit that I am sensitive to the comparison. The ape comparison is bothersome, but a monkey is a much more annoying association, perhaps because I do chatter a bit. I was a talker in my own language, but the English language opened up all manner of possibilities, and I have most likely taken advantage of all of them multiple times.

That said, even I should know it's bad storytelling to stop a story in the midst of momentum when someone enters into the wheelhouse with a gun, and especially since I'm trying to describe true events and let you know how things went. But there's that chattering problem I just told you about. I may go off on a tangent at any moment; I think all the coffee I drink adds to it.

I would like to say there was a big heroic moment that occurred, an immediate battle for the gun, but to be honest, we were all as stunned as if we had awakened to see the sunrise was blue. Red pointed the gun and fired. The shot hit The Big Guy in the stomach. The Big Guy dropped like a pig in the slaughterhouse. Red fired again, at me, but I was moving and the shot tore through the windshield. The Woman dropped to her knee, grabbed The Big Guy's head, lifted it up. Everyone else hit the floor. It sounded like a wash woman had dropped wet laundry in there.

As I said, I was moving. I went crazy. In that moment everything about me that was civilized went out that hole in the windshield, same as the bullet that blew it open. I sprang forward and grabbed Red as he fired. I felt a pain like a hot iron against my side, and then I had Red by the head with both hands, lifting him off his feet. I threw him toward the side windows, one of those that wasn't open. He hit with such force the glass shattered into thousands of sun-winked stars; he went right through the opening his body made, out into the wind, the revolver flying from his hand as if it had gone to roost.

I jumped to the window, looked down.

THE APE MAN'S BROTHER

He had fallen onto the top wing of one of the biplanes below, and was swinging himself to the lower wing on the port side of the craft. I suspected he was planning to open the cockpit, release the clamp with the wrench that was inside for just such a purpose, and try and fly away. I doubted he had any real flight knowledge, but we were still high enough over the lost world he might well have glided to the ground, and to safety. He might even try to fly the plane into the zeppelin if he had any understanding of how the craft worked. I couldn't take any chances.

●●●

I went through that gap in the broken window and clung to one of the metal windshield struts. There was a coiled rope ladder to the right of me where there was a door that led out to it and the plane below. I could have climbed back inside and gone out the door and used the ladder, but I hadn't become that civilized. I kicked off my toeless house shoes, stretched my leg way out and kicked the ladder loose. It tumbled down until it was even with the bottom wing of the biplane. By this time Red had managed to reach the cockpit, had lifted it up, and was climbing into the plane.

I leaped and grabbed the ladder, was down it and onto the bottom wing of that plane faster than someone on the ground could have looked up and seen me and said, "Is that a monkey or a man in a wool jacket up there?"

What I didn't expect was for him not to be in the cockpit. He had opened it and taken out the wrench, and was standing on the bottom wing, clinging with one hand to a wing strut, and in the other he had that wrench. He hit me with it. It was a glancing blow, but it knocked me off the wing. I was able to twist my body and catch the edge of the wing. He scooted forward and stomped one of my hands, hard. I swung out, grabbed the plane's propeller, which of course was stationary, scrambled along it, up over the nose of the plane, and back onto the bottom wing. He was gone. The ladder was visible and it was vibrating. He was going back up.

I don't know if he was truly bug-shit crazy, or just afraid he hadn't finished the job on The Big Guy. Or maybe he wanted to do The Woman harm. Maybe he wasn't thinking at all, just working off instinct. I scrambled up after him.

Feeling the pull of my weight below, he pivoted and saw me. He had stuck the wrench in his back pocket, and now, hanging on with one hand, he grabbed hold of it with his free hand. As I came close enough to grab his ankle, he leaned down and tried to hit me with the wrench. I dodged, grabbed at the weapon and ripped it from his hand. It was such a violent motion I lost my grip on the ladder. I spun out and landed on the top wing of the biplane with enough force to knock the breath out of me.

I got my air quickly, hustled to my feet, glanced down and saw the earth was coming up fast. In all of the confusion, something had gone wrong up in the wheel-house. I leaped off the wing and snatched at the ladder, climbed up to the broken window glass just in time to see that the bullet that had grazed me had caught Dr. Rice. I hadn't noticed this before I went out the window. Dr. Rice was down, not moving. Bowen Tyler was struggling at the wheel, which looked bent. Keep in mind that while it takes me time to describe all this, it all occurred rather quickly. I assumed Dr. Rice, after being shot, had fallen into the wheel with such force that his weight had done something to it. Maybe the bullet that had grazed me and killed him had gone through him and done damage to the control panel. I can't honestly say, but the craft was flying erratically. I could hear the rear propellers cutting out. The great gas bag was starting to dip its nose. The Big Guy was on his feet. He had ripped off his shirt, and his stomach was covered in blood. He was a little wobbly. The Woman clutched his huge arm, as if to help. The Big Guy pulled free of her just as I was trying to climb through the window after Red.

Red went at The Big Guy. He swung the wrench. The Big Guy, wounded as he was, dodged it and grabbed Red's arm. There was a cracking sound, like the weight of heavy ice breaking a rotten limb, then there was a savage yell from The Big Guy; the sort of war cry that would have made that actor who played him in the movies crap himself.

And then I, one foot hanging through the broken window, was splattered in blood, and so was everyone else. It

was like a geyser full of red plum juice had erupted. The reason for this wasn't only that The Big Guy had twisted Red's arm off at the elbow and it was spurting, but as they went down together in a tangle of limbs and blood, The Big Guy bit out Red's throat with a wild gnash of his teeth. You could hear flesh ripping like someone tearing old bed sheets. The Big Guy sprang to his feet, leaped up and down on Red a few times, put a foot on Red's destroyed and bloody throat, bent down and grabbed that flame-head, and yanked that sucker off as easy as jerking a cork out of a bottle with a wine screw.

This would have held our attention longer had not Bowen said, "I can't lift it."

He was talking about the zeppelin. It was dropping fast. I had just managed to climb completely through the gap in the window (which should give you some idea how fast The Big Guy took care of Red) when it listed to starboard, then turned completely over. I hit the roof of the wheelhouse, which had become my floor, glimpsed through the windshield at a huge, leathery, flying beast grabbing at the zeppelin with its claws, screeching loudly. I thought, perfect. If it wasn't for bad luck we'd have no luck at all.

I don't remember much after that.

[15]

I never knew when we hit. Or at least I don't remember it. Perhaps it was the impact that knocked that part of my memory away.

When I awoke the wheelhouse was wadded up around me as if I was a chocolate in tissue paper. The zeppelin had landed on its top; it had stayed completely turned over. I was close to one of the windshields, which had lost all its glass, and managed my way through it, receiving only minor cuts. I got hold of one of the support ropes that contained the gas bag, worked my way briskly to the ground. The leather-winged monster, or at least part of him, was poking out from under the gas bag, dead. I could hear helium leaking from the zeppelin like a slow fart from a grandma. We had been low enough to the ground, that with the zeppelin turning over, the gas bag itself had cushioned our fall. It was still a hell of a drop.

No sooner was I on the ground than it occurred to me that I had left The Big Guy and The Woman in the wheelhouse, or what was left of it. I was about to climb back, when I heard The Woman call out to me. Just hearing her caused a sudden rush of memories to flood through me; our picnics, our talks, sitting on the hotel balcony with a glass of wine or a cup of coffee, screwing like mongooses.

I turned and saw her kneeling over The Big Guy. They had been thrown free of the crash. Bowen Tyler was nearby, sitting up, looking dazed, a hand to his bleeding head. I hurried over to The Woman and The Big Guy. The Big Guy wasn't moving. I pushed her aside and put my head to his chest, peeled back an eye lid and looked at his eye.

"He's still alive," I said. "I'll see if I can find some first aid."

Most everything that had been in the cabins and the storage rooms was scattered about on the ground. I scurried amongst it all, running on all fours as I did in the old days, and quickly came across the small trunk that contained our medical supplies. I dragged it over to where The Big Guy lay. I tore the locked lid off as easy as you might rip the top off a box of cereal. I still had my strength.

To make a long story short, I bandaged him up. The bullet had hit him in the stomach, and there isn't a much worse wound, normally, but with the bullet having gone through him, and by some miracle not having destroyed anything major, and with him having such incredible recuperative powers... Well, let me make this story even shorter. He was going to live.

THE APE MAN'S BROTHER

Our first order of business was we buried Dr. Rice and all the others who had died on the zeppelin; that was everyone but those I've mentioned. I dragged what was left of Red off a good distance from us and each day I would watch the huge buzzards of our world descend on him and finish off what was left of him. I stopped there nightly where he was rotting and being eaten away to piss on his corpse. I never did find his head.

We ended up staying near the wreckage of the zeppelins for a few days to give The Big Guy time to grow stronger. We had found and broken out the firearms for safety. Bowen, like The Woman, had only minor injuries. While we waited, all manner of beasts showed up, as I knew they would. With our weapons, and having built a large fire, we were able to keep them at bay, as well as provide ourselves with breakfast, lunch and dinner.

Better yet, I knew where we were. It was about a three day walk from where my people congregated. We made a litter, put The Big Guy on it, and started out. It took about five days. It was slower than three days with me and Bowen having to carry The Big Guy, who was no feather, let me tell you. We also had to stop and change bandages. Those ran out after day two, but there were plenty of large leaves, some of which could soak up blood as fine as cotton. I had also sewn his belly shut with a large thorn and some fibers from a plant I knew made good stout thread. Anyway, we took five days to reach my country, across the savanna and deep into the jungle.

I began to see our people before we arrived at my old homeland. They were up in the trees, hiding carefully at the edge of the narrow trail, watching. I actually recognized one of them, and in my own language, said, "Hey, picking many fleas?"

It's a kind of a greeting we have.

My old friend came out of the brush then, a little nervous. He said my name. I agreed that it was indeed me. He recognized The Big Guy, and though The Big Guy may have fallen into our midst, he was considered one of us. More of my people melted out of the jungle and onto the trail. Bowen looked nervous, but I reassured him.

That's how we came to spend about six months among my people. The Big Guy healed up quickly. Within what I estimate to be about six weeks he was fine. We even went hunting together like in the old days, and though I had lost the taste for our hairy females, what the hell, I humped a few of them; it seemed the least I could do so that no one might think I had gotten too high above my raising.

The Woman, who I thought might find this a pretty uncomfortable world once she was introduced to it with the idea of staying, fooled me. She took to it like a cow to grass. Like The Big Guy, she had abandoned her clothes, and had gone native. I got to tell you, she looked fine like that, brown-skinned and sweat-glazed, her hair standing out from her head like an electrified halo.

She and The Big Guy even built a home. A tree house. Constructed between two massive trees with spreading limbs and great overhead foliage so thick it could hold off a pretty serious rain. Not that it mattered. The Big Guy put a thatched roof on their house, and those digs were quite large for being built so quickly; four big rooms and a veranda that ran all the way around. The Big Guy even rigged up some kind of device that held rain water and could be tapped into for drinking, and bathing if they chose, though most of their bathing they did in the nearby rivers, streams or ponds. His time in the civilized world had made more of an impact on him that I expected, and his ability to construct that house out of native materials surprised me. When we had lived here in the past, a crook in a tree was good enough for us, but now, with The Woman, he wanted to give her the best of both worlds. I think another thing that made it easier for her was that she didn't really have any family to go home to. Her father, Dr. Rice was the end of it. Her mother had died when she was a child. Dr. Rice had raised her. I think she liked the idea of being near his grave.

As I have said, I had grown to like civilization, and missed it. Bowen was ready to go home as well. So on a cool night with all of us up in the tree house, drinking wine we had gone back and rescued from the zeppelin crash (surprisingly most of the bottles had survived), I said what I had dreaded to say. Me and Bowen were going home.

The zeppelin was beyond repair, but the biplanes, both of them, were in fine shape. We would have to release them from the zeppelin and turn them over on their wheels, but I thought with the help of a lot of my people, that could be done. A plane couldn't carry us all the way back to America, but Bowen had charted out the possibility of Greenland, the place The Big Guy's folks had flown from. It was a close possibility, and he wasn't sure we could make it, but since there were a couple of intact cans of gas along with the planes' filled reservoir, and me being quite nimble and able to gas it up in flight by means of a can and hose and good strong rope, we thought there was a good chance we could manage it that far. I reminded Bowen that The Big Guy's parents had made it from Greenland to here, and that gave me hope. He reminded me the wind patterns were different, and we would be pushing against the wind in spots. Still, we missed home bad enough we were willing to give it a try.

The Big Guy cried. I mean he cried, just let loose with a howl and started leaking tears. He clutched me to him, and damn near broke me. He begged me to stay, but I was stalwart in my plans, and told him so. The Woman cried and hugged me to her naked body as well. I clung to her as long as I could without getting an erection. I thought, considering past events, that would be bad form. Another thing, I couldn't stay close to her for much longer because the old feelings still existed, and I didn't want anything to fan that little blaze into a fire.

Bowen shook hands with them, went on down. I stayed for one last drink of wine. I should add that I was drinking and The Woman was drinking, but The Big

Guy was not. He had sworn off the stuff forever, in any shape or form. He drank a kind of coffee made from jungle nuts. It was pretty awful, and hard to get used to. It tasted to me as if it were goat shit boiled in sewer water, but he had a hankering for it and drank it by the cups.

When we had our drinks, I said, "You know, there's something I feel I must tell you." I told them about the serum, and that The Big Guy had, at least according to Dr. Rice, received it when he was a child, that it gave him everlasting life, and that he might remain as he was forever, provided he wasn't killed or got some kind of disease. I explained this as best I could, and The Big Guy sat there mulling it over. The Woman let out her breath and jerked a hand to her mouth. "He won't age. And I will?"

I nodded.

She buried her face in her hands.

I said, "I think there might be a way where you can both continue to be as you are now."

The Woman peeked through her fingers. "Really?"

"Maybe."

I had brought a little box with me that night, along with the wine, and now I opened it. Inside were items from the medical supplies. Hypodermic needles and big glass syringes.

I put a needle in a syringe. I said, "If I can draw some of The Big Guy's blood, and then put that blood in you, it may serve as a serum for you as well. I can't guarantee it, but we can try. It's one of your father's theories."

"He told you all of this," she said.

"He did. Me and him, we got along well."

"I knew you did," she said, "but this… It's amazing."

"I can't guarantee it will work," I said. "But I thought we should try."

"Oh, my heavens," The Woman said. "We must. The idea of growing old, and losing him… I can't face it."

"Your age doesn't matter," said The Big Guy, which was spoken like someone who had never fucked an old lady. I am not suggesting that I have… Oh, hell. A few times, at fundraisers for charities back in the States.

"You should inject yourself as well," said The Woman to me.

"I can try," I said, but Dr. Rice and I had discussed this, and it was possible that I was a different enough species it might not take. I didn't mention that to them, but as you can tell, sitting here with me, my fur as gray as cigar ash, it didn't work.

I drew The Big Guy's blood into the needle, gave a shot of it to The Woman, in the rump, which was a pleasant experience for me, if not her. When it was done, I put the medical tools away, hugged them both, and climbed down to sleep until the break of light. That was when Bowen and I would start our trip to Greenland, and then home. Or we would crash in the ocean when our fuel ran out. I was, of course, hoping for the former.

[16]

We didn't make it to Greenland. We crashed in the ocean, and damned if the plane didn't float for a full day and night, and only began to sink the next day. By then we had spotted a steamer and it had spotted us. We were rescued by the crew, and as the ship was on its way to New York City, we were saved.

So, now, here I am, in my modest apartment, quite aged, having never gone back to my lost world. For the most part, my money is gone, except for a little old age pension, which, of course, is why I have to charge you for the pleasure or my company. And need I mention that I prefer cash, not a check?

Bowen died some fifteen years ago of a heart attack. Dr. Rice is now a figure of ridicule, as am I and The Big Guy. Who we were, what we did, and where we came from, has been poorly remembered, taken out of context, or forgotten. What is remembered has been mixed with lies. People these days believe more than ever that our story is nothing more than a swindle.

The entire world from which we came, all that happened to us, is now thought to have been a big fat lie, that I am a man with a strange, hairy condition, and nothing more. Finally that lion screwing event has become even better known, and with the crassness that has become the Americas, it is now shown at a number of venues, and presented frame by frame in numerous magazines. It has robbed The Big Guy of what reputation he once had, and with the money mostly played out from our films, both our reputations have taken a greater hit. Money keeps the paint fresh. When it plays out, the paint begins to peel.

It's not all bad. Explorers say there is no such place as we claimed those years ago. There are also plenty who have said my insistence on its existence is merely senility, that I have come to believe the story myself. This protects The Big Guy, and I know you don't believe me either. I can see it in your eyes.

That's okay. I have aged. The serum didn't work on me. I think it has to do with a different number of chromosomes or something. Yet, I am not senile. I have described it as it was. My mind still works and I still like to visit the ladies. It's probably a good thing that my species can't reproduce with yours, or the world would be filled with hairy folks with long toes.

I am growing tired. I doubt there is anything else left to say that is worth saying. I sit here and remember the old days, and from time to time wonder if I made the right decision to come back to civilization. It's not a thought that occupies a lot of my time, however. I am for the most part quite happy being civilized; in my old world the weak, the tired, and the wounded die young.

Looking back, it's strange the way The Big Guy's path crossed mine. Stranger yet, the ape has become the man, and the man has become the ape. I was fortunate to know him, and to know The Woman.

I wonder what happened to them. Did the injection I gave her work? Are they still alive in the jungles of the lost world, hale and hearty, dwelling in their tree house, having adventures, lying together, loving together until the end of time?

It is certainly nice to think so.